PEA
SOUP
AND
SEA SERPENTS

PEA SOUP AND SEA SERPENTS

Written and illustrated by
WILLIAM SCHRODER

Lothrop, Lee & Shepard Company
A Division of William Morrow & Company, Inc. • New York

To **Burt,**
Mary
and **Barbara**

2   3   4   5   6   7   8   9   10

Library of Congress Cataloging in Publication Data
Schroder, William E
    Pea soup and sea serpents.
    SUMMARY: Two young boys set off to hunt for sea serpents but are
foiled by thick fog.
    [1. Fog—Fiction] I. Title.
PZ7.S3794Pe   [E]   76-44405
ISBN 0-688-41785-X   ISBN 0-688-51785-4 lib. bdg.

Norton and Atherton decided
to hunt for sea serpents.

"We will need a rope to tie it up, should we capture one," said Atherton.

"And a bucket to carry it in," said Norton.

"Assuming it is not too large," said Atherton.

"How big could it be if it lives in a pond?" asked Norton.

"It is foggy," said Atherton.
"Like pea soup," said Norton.
"That will make it easier to take the monster by surprise," said Atherton.

Norton said, "My glasses are getting all misty."

"Do you see any sea serpents?"
asked Norton.
"I believe they are very shy beasts,"
said Atherton.
"I see," said Norton.
"We will take out the boat," said Atherton.
"Do you know much about boats?" asked Norton.
"Not a great deal," said Atherton.
"Neither do I," said Norton.
"Then we should put on the life jackets,"
said Atherton.
"Yes," said Norton.

"Cast off!" said Atherton.

"Aye, aye," said Norton.

"How far are we from shore?" asked Norton.
"I cannot see the shore," replied Atherton.
"I can barely see the water," said Norton.

"It certainly is quiet," said Norton.
"That is because there is nobody about today,"
said Atherton.
"True," said Norton.

"The boat is rocking," said Norton.

"The sea is getting choppy," said Atherton.

"Maybe there is a storm coming up," said Norton.

"This is an unfortunate situation,"
said Atherton.

"Man overboard!" said Atherton.

"Men overboard!" said Norton.

"At least the water is not cold," said Norton.
"I think we should swim to shore,"
said Atherton.
"Where is it?" asked Norton.

"Stay near me so you do not get lost,"
said Atherton.
"Where are you?" asked Norton.
"Here I am," said Atherton.
"Ah," said Norton.

"I am being lifted out of the water,"
said Norton.
"Perhaps our boat has come up beneath us,"
said Atherton.
"Whatever is under me does not feel like
a boat," said Norton.
"What else could it be?" asked Atherton.
"We are moving, unless I am greatly mistaken,"
said Norton.
"Perhaps there is a strong wind pushing us,"
said Atherton.
"Perhaps," said Norton.

"I wonder where we are headed," said Norton.
"To shore, I hope," said Atherton.
"I hope so too," said Norton.

"That was a rough landing," said Atherton.
"Rough indeed," said Norton.
"Are you all right?" asked Atherton.
"I am all right," said Norton. "I wonder
if the boat is damaged."

"I cannot see the boat," said Norton.

"Neither can I," said Atherton.

"Perhaps we should go home and change into dry clothes."

"Perhaps we will find a sea serpent on another occasion," said Atherton.
"When it is less foggy," added Norton.
"If there are any to find in a pond," said Atherton, and he sneezed.

WILLIAM SCHRODER is a costume and set designer who received his B.A. at Wesleyan University in Middletown, Connecticut. He has shown his artistic talent in all kinds of theatrical productions, from Shakespeare to modern drama, in regional theater and national tours, as well as on Broadway. Mr. Schroder lives in New York City. *Pea Soup and Sea Serpents* is his first book.